ESTE LIVRO PERTENCE A

________________________

AUTHENTIC GAMES
TESOURO PERDIDO
astral cultural

**Produção editorial** Aline Santos, Bárbara Gatti, Fernanda Costa, Jaqueline Lopes, Mariana Rodrigueiro, Natália Ortega, Paula Santana/ Colaboradora, Renan Oliveira e Tâmizi Ribeiro
**Capa** Agência MOV e Aline Santos **Ilustração** VicTycoon
**Ilustrações personagens** VicTycoon e Pepeu404
**Ilustrações cenário** Anna.zabella/shutterstock, Astira/shutterstock, ClassicVector/shutterstock, elenabsl/shutterstock,elenabsl/ shutterstock, Elvetica/shutterstock, Igogosha/shutterstock, Mooi Design/shutterstock, Nearbirds/shutterstock, PixelChoice/ shutterstock, StockVectorsIllustrations/shutterstock, Unitone Vector/shutterstock, Vectorpocket/shutterstock, vectorpouch/ shutterstock, VVadyab Pico/shutterstock, Yevheniia Rodina/ shutterstock
**Fotos do autor** Leca Novo
**Avaliação pedagógica** Luciana Ribeiro Salomão

Dados Internacionais de Catalogação na Publicação (CIP)
Angélica Ilacqua CRB-8/7057

---

T83a Túlio, Marco
AuthenticGames: tesouro perdido / Marco Túlio; [ilustrações de VicTycoon] — Bauru, SP: Astral Cultural, 2021.
48 p.: il., color.

ISBN: 978-65-5566-038-8

1. Literatura infantojuvenil 2. Minecraft (jogo) - Ficção infantojuvenil I. Título II. VicTycoon

20-2881

CDD 028.5

---

Índice para catálogo sistemático:
1. Literatura infantojuveni

ASTRAL CULTURAL EDITORA LTDA

BAURU
Av. Duque de Caxias 11-70, 8° andar
CEP 17012-151
Telefone: (14) 3235-3878
Fax: (14) 3235-3879

SÃO PAULO
Rua Helena 140, sala 13
1° andar, Vila Olímpia
CEP 04552-050

E-mail: contato@astralcultural.com.br

# BEM-VINDOS À MINHA COLEÇÃO!

Maninhos e maninhas, estejam preparados para encarar mais uma aventura! A coleção AuthenticGames conta com doze histórias incríveis para se divertir e aprender muito comigo e com minha turma. Em cada livro, vamos levar bons exemplos e importantes lições para serem praticadas no dia a dia. Aqui, você vai saber sobre a importância de estarmos sempre alegres e ajudarmos os amigos a manterem a felicidade. Pode parecer difícil, mas não é. Vamos lá?

# I

# UMA NOTÍCIA INESPERADA

**Aquela notícia havia pegado todo** mundo de surpresa: Gui, um amigo da galera que estudava em outra sala, mas jogava futebol junto com eles, mudaria de cidade. Na saída da escola, ele chamou todo mundo para dar a notícia e, pelas carinhas, todos ficaram tristes.

— Mas e o futebol? Não podemos jogar sem o nosso goleiro! O time vai ficar desfalcado. — Authentic disse, chateado.

— Nós não estávamos prontos para essa notícia, não... E as disputas de videogame aos domingos? — Baixa falou, triste.

— Poxa, gente. Eu estou tão triste quanto vocês... Mas não tem o que fazer, minha mãe foi promovida no trabalho e vamos ter mesmo que nos mudar, mas a cidade nova não é muito longe... — Gui tentou animar o pessoal.

— Fico muito feliz pela sua mãe, Gui! Já podemos planejar uma visita nas férias? — Lydia tentou levantar o astral da turma.

— Claro! Vai ser incrível receber vocês! — Gui respondeu, empolgado.

— Se o seu novo time de futebol competir com a gente, não vou dar moleza, hein? — Reverso disse, colocando a mão no ombro do amigo e dando risada.

— Calma aí, Reverso! Eu nem me mudei ainda e você já está falando isso? — Gui deu uma risadinha sem graça.

— Ah, é bom te deixar preparado — Baixa completou.

— Bom, não podemos controlar tudo... Mas mudanças não são ruins, você vai ver só! — Authentic tentou animá-lo.

— Você vai se esquecer da gente rapidinho — disse Reverso.

— Nããããão! Eu nunca vou me esquecer de vocês! — gritou Gui.

Apesar da notícia, os amigos estavam tentando não ficar tristes, o motivo da mudança de Gui era muito bom para a família dele e seria proveitoso para ele também. Era difícil manter a alegria naquele momento, mas não impossível.

Secreto
2
O
PLANO
SECRETO

**A turma se reuniu na casa de Authentic** logo que receberam a notícia. Eles precisavam de um plano para aquela mudança ser o mais alegre possível, mas ainda não sabiam como fariam isso. O jeito era pensar juntos.

— E se nós fizermos uma festa de despedida? — sugeriu Authentic.

— Uma ótima ideia, Authentic! Mas precisamos de mais... Só a festa parece pouco, não? — disse Baixa.

— Precisamos de algo que o Gui possa levar, além das memórias... — Lydia falou.

— Que pensamento profundo, Lydia! — Reverso brincou. — Mas o que seria? Um presente?

— Acho que, para ser especial, precisamos fazer o presente... — Authentic sugeriu.

— Que missão difícil! — reclamou Baixa. — Não sei nem por onde começar... Alguém tem mais alguma ideia?

— Não... Acho que podemos pesquisar... — disse Lydia. — Authentic, onde está seu notebook?

— Vou buscar para você! — Authentic respondeu, indo em direção ao quarto.

Quando Authentic pegou o notebook, seus olhos passaram por alguns livros. Foi então que ele se lembrou de um sobre tesouros preciosos perdidos e teve uma ideia, grande o suficiente para cada um fazer sua parte nesse processo. Gui iria adorar, Authentic não tinha dúvidas.

3
A
IDEIA
PERFEITA

**Assim que voltou para a sala, Authentic** contou a ideia que teve: eles escreveriam várias cartas sobre os momentos que eles passaram juntos na escola, no futebol, entre outras coisas. Além disso, eles imprimiriam fotos, colocariam tudo em um baú e fariam uma caça ao tesouro na festa de despedida.

— Que ideia incrível, Authentic! — disse Baixa. — Já quero começar a escrever.

— Eu também! — Lydia se animou.

— Mas e o baú? Onde vamos achar um? — Reverso perguntou.

— Nós podemos fazer também! Com a ajuda do meu pai, é claro — Authentic sugeriu. — Se nós fizermos tudo, vai ficar ainda mais especial.

— Você tem razão, Authentic — Baixa concordou. — Agora que resolvemos o presente, precisamos começar a pensar na festa.

— Boa, Baixa! Mas onde vamos fazer uma festa que será possível esconder um baú? — Reverso ficou pensativo.

— Não tinha pensado nisso... — Authentic respondeu.

— Calma, pessoal! Vamos conseguir dar um jeito nisso também — Baixa disse.

— É... Essa não é uma tarefa impossível — Reverso completou. — E acho que já sei o que vou escrever! Também tenho algumas fotos do time de futebol, vão ficar muito legais.

— O primeiro campeonato que ganhamos com ele no time, lembra? — Authentic recordou.

— Aquele jogo foi difícil, mas foi uma vitória que vale a pena lembrar — Reverso completou.

4
UMA
MISSÃO
POSSÍVEL

**A galera deixou de lado a tristeza da** mudança de Gui e começou a focar em coisas boas, afinal, eles não perderiam o amigo, ganhariam mais um lugar para visitar e, quem sabe, novos amigos nessas viagens.

— Terminei minha carta! — disse Authentic.

— Eu também! Mas preciso procurar mais coisas para colocar no baú, quero que o Gui se lembre mais de mim — Baixa falou, rindo.

— Bom saber, Baixa... Vou escrever aqui na minha pedindo para ele se lembrar mais de mim... — brincou Reverso.

Lydia estava organizando a lista da festa, mandando mensagem para que outros amigos de Gui também escrevessem cartinhas para ele e pedindo segredo. Ela não queria que alguém acabasse estragando a surpresa.

Authentic foi falar com seu pai, contou a ideia e pediu ajuda para construírem um baú bem bonito e resistente. O pai adorou e foi logo ajudar a turminha. Mas, apesar de todos os detalhes, ainda faltava decidir algo muito importante: o local da festa e onde estaria escondido o baú.

— Gente! Já sei o que podemos fazer! — disse Authentic, empolgado. — Nós podemos espalhar pistas por todos os lugares que o Gui costuma ir aqui na cidade... A escola, o campo de futebol, a sorveteria...

— Que ideia incrível, Authentic! Tá inspirado hoje, hein, cara? — comentou Baixa.

— Então, vocês topam? — Authentic perguntou, olhando para os amigos que pareciam animados com a ideia.

— Claro, Authentic! — Lydia respondeu imediatamente.

— Só se for agora! O que precisamos fazer? — Reverso também topou o plano.

— Acho que já sei por onde podemos começar! — disse Authentic.

# 5

# UM CONVITE ESPECIAL

Com a ideia de Authentic em mente, os amigos se juntaram no dia seguinte após a aula e preparam as pistas para a caça ao tesouro. Porém, como tudo era segredo, eles precisaram inventar uma desculpa para não saírem com Gui naquela tarde.

— Coitado, ele ficou tão chateado quando falamos que não podíamos sair com ele depois da aula — disse Authentic, escrevendo uma das pistas.

— Mas foi por um bom motivo, ele vai entender quando souber — Baixa completou, também escrevendo uma das pistas.

— Vai ficar tudo tão lindo, gente! Estou emocionada — Lydia disse, terminando de montar o baú com as recordações.

— Ele, com certeza, vai ficar muito feliz, tanto quanto nós estamos — Authentic falou.

Tudo estava pronto para a festa de despedida surpresa no final de semana. A turma havia combinado com os pais de Gui para eles esconderem o baú, eles seriam os responsáveis pelo tesouro. Os pais adoraram a ideia e ficaram muito felizes com tanto carinho. Para que Gui não descobrisse, Authentic o chamou para jogar videogame, e, então, o plano seria colocado em prática.

Quando os meninos estavam na sala, jogando videogame, Baixa chegou com um envelope e entregou para Gui.

— E aí, Baixa? Veio jogar com a gente? — perguntou Gui.

— Não! Vim te entregar este envelope aqui — Baixa respondeu, entregando o papel a ele.

— O que é isso? Um convite? — Gui olhou, curioso.

— Você só vai saber depois de ler! Abra! — respondeu Baixa, empolgado com o início da caça ao tesouro.

— Quanto mistério — Gui falou, olhando para Authentic e para Baixa.

Authentic e Baixa olhavam de volta para o amigo, muito animados. Depois de ler, Gui disse:

— Hmmm... Aqui diz para eu ir até a sorveteria, vamos?

6

# O TESOURO PERDIDO

**Quando chegaram à sorveteria, Lydia** entregou outro envelope para Gui. Dessa vez, ele deveria ir até o campo de futebol da cidade.

— Estou ficando curioso com esses envelopes! O que vocês aprontaram? — Gui olhou para os amigos, empolgado.

— Nada, não! — Authentic riu. — Vamos, estamos perdendo tempo!

E, assim, eles seguiram juntos para o campo de futebol, em busca de mais uma pista.

Quando chegaram lá, Reverso entregou mais uma pista, que os levava até a escola. Os amigos estavam felizes ao notarem que o plano estava funcionando e, Gui parecia muito alegre com tudo aquilo.

— Vocês não vão me dar nenhuma dica, gente? — Gui tentou mais uma vez.

— Ué, as pistas já são as dicas, Gui! — Authentic disse. — Mais que isso não vale!

Na escola, a última pista estava em sua carteira, na sala de aula. E ela o mandava direto para o bosque da cidade. Quando chegaram lá, todos os amigos de Gui estavam o esperando, e ele ficou surpreso com aquilo. Mas aquele ainda não era o destino final.

— Ei, não acabou ainda, não! — disse Authentic. — Aqui está o último envelope.

Assim que leu a última pista, Gui foi direto para o parque, e encontrou um lugar marcado com X no chão, perto do escorregador. Na mesma hora, ele pegou uma pá que estava ao lado do escorregador e começou a cavar. Gui ficou surpreso e muito feliz quando viu um baú. Quando abriu, ficou impressionado ao ver diversas cartas dos amigos, fotos, desenhos e até mesmo chocolates.

— Muito obrigado, estou emocionado!

— Você merece, Gui — Baixa falou, dando um abraço no amigo.

— A gente sabe que mudanças podem não ser fáceis, mas os amigos podem ajudar a deixar esse momento mais leve — disse Authentic.

— E nosso verdadeiro tesouro, no fim, são as nossas amizades — Lydia completou.

— Foi por isso que vocês não puderam jogar videogame ontem? — perguntou Gui.

— Sim, estávamos preparando tudo e não queríamos estragar a surpresa — Authentic respondeu.

— Pela primeira vez, estou muito feliz que vocês tenham recusado um convite para jogar videogame — Gui disse, rindo.

— E nós ficamos felizes por você ter gostado da surpresa — Baixa falou.

— Eu amei! É uma alegria imensa ter vocês como amigos, não sei nem como agradecer tanto carinho.

— Pode nos agradecer nas férias, quando formos na sua casa! — disse Authentic.

— Vocês estão mais do que convidados para me visitar, galera! — disse Gui, dando um hi-5 com Authentic e Baixa. — Sempre que quiserem. Mas e aí, vamos aproveitar a festa agora?

— CLAAAARO! — todos responderam, empolgados.

E foram aproveitar a festa, sabendo que aquela não seria a última vez que veriam Gui, eles ainda teriam muitas aventuras juntos.

7

# UMA VIAGEM DE FÉRIAS

**Alguns meses se passaram desde a** mudança de Gui para outra cidade. O campeonato de futebol sem ele não havia sido o mesmo, mas Lydia sempre dava um jeito de deixar o amigo mais perto da galera com chamadas de vídeo diretamente da arquibancada. Agora, finalmente havia chegado a tal viagem que eles haviam combinado.

— Vamos, pessoal! Desse jeito a gente só chega lá na semana que vem — apressou Authentic.

— Pronto, Authentic! Todo mundo pronto por aqui! — disse Baixa, arrastando sua mala pela calçada.

O pai de Authentic havia combinado de levar a turminha para visitar Gui e passar alguns dias por lá. Tudo estava de acordo com os pais do amigo, é claro. Ele estava alegre por ver toda a empolgação do pessoal com a viagem, a turma estava com muita saudade.

— Vamos, Baixa! Eu te ajudo a colocar a sua mala no carro — disse Authentic. — Só está faltando a sua.

— Obrigado! — agradeceu Baixa.

Assim que terminaram de organizar tudo, eles partiram em direção à casa de Gui. Animados e contentes, foram cantando e conversando durante toda a viagem e, assim, o tempo passou rapidinho. Quando notaram, já estavam na porta da casa do amigo, tocando a campainha.

— Olha só vocês! Finalmente chegaram! Achei que não viriam mais — disse Gui ao abrir a porta.

— Claro que não! Estamos planejando essa viagem há meses, até parece que não íamos vir te ver! — Authentic correu para abraçar Gui.

— É bom demais ver todo mundo reunido assim! — Lydia falou, emocionada, observando toda a cena com os amigos juntos.

— Vem, galera! Vamos entrando! A minha mãe preparou um almoço muito especial — Gui comentou, colocando as mãos na barriga.

— Hmmm... Acho que já sabemos qual vai ser a melhor parte dessa viagem! — respondeu Baixa, fazendo todo mundo rir.

Os amigos sabiam que aquela aventura, na verdade, só estava começando. E eles estavam muito contentes por estarem ali, partilhando mais um momento com o maior tesouro que se pode ter na vida: os amigos.

# FALA, GALERA, BELEZA?

**AQUI QUEM FALA É O AUTHENTIC!**

Nesta história, vimos a importância de manter a alegria, pois ela é contagiante! Nem sempre podemos controlar tudo o que acontece em nossa volta. A mudança de um amigo para uma outra cidade pode ser uma situação chata a princípio, mas a amizade supera qualquer distância. Aqui, a alegria esteve presente o tempo todo, mesmo quando estávamos tristes, pois a nossa principal meta era deixar nosso amigo feliz e mostrar que ele sempre poderia contar com a gente. E você, já mostrou para um amigo o quanto ele é especial?

# SOBRE O AUTOR

Marco Túlio, o nome por trás da marca AuthenticGames, é sucesso dentro e fora do YouTube! Com um currículo de peso, o youtuber e empresário já viajou por todo o país com seu show, tem em sua estante o Prêmio Jovem Brasileiro e, em 2019, entrou para lista FORBES UNDER 30. Mas as coisas não param por aí... Marco Túlio é um dos autores mais vendidos do país, com mais de 1 milhão de livros vendidos! Agora, seguindo em sua jornada pelo mundo da ficção, ele lança uma nova série de livros que pretende passar às crianças bons valores e importantes lições de vida.

**Primeira edição** (fevereiro/2021)
**Papel de miolo** Offset 90g
**Tipografias** Pixel Operator e Molot Regular
**Gráfica** IPSIS

TWENTIETH CENTURY FOX PRESENTS A DAVIS ENTERTAINMENT COMPANY / BRANDYWINE PRODUCTION A PAUL W. S. ANDERSON FILM "ALIEN VS. PREDATOR" SANAA LATHAN RAOUL BOVA LANCE HENRIKSEN EWEN BREMNER COSTUME DESIGNER MAGALI GUIDASCI MUSIC BY HARALD KLOSER CREATURE EFFECTS DESIGNED AND CREATED BY ALEC GILLIS AND TOM WOODRUFF, JR. VISUAL EFFECTS SUPERVISOR JOHN BRUNO FILM EDITOR ALEXANDER BERNER PRODUCTION DESIGNER RICHARD BRIDGLAND DIRECTOR OF PHOTOGRAPHY DAVID JOHNSON CO-PRODUCER CHRIS SYMES EXECUTIVE PRODUCERS WYCK GODFREY THOMAS M. HAMMEL MIKE RICHARDSON PRODUCED BY JOHN DAVIS GORDON CARROLL DAVID GILER AND WALTER HILL BASED ON THE "ALIEN" CHARACTERS CREATED BY DAN O'BANNON AND RONALD SHUSETT AND THE "PREDATOR" CHARACTERS CREATED BY JIM THOMAS & JOHN THOMAS SCREEN STORY BY PAUL W. S. ANDERSON AND DAN O'BANNON & RONALD SHUSETT SCREENPLAY BY PAUL W. S. ANDERSON DIRECTED BY PAUL W. S. ANDERSON

PG-13 PARENTS STRONGLY CAUTIONED
Some Material May Be Inappropriate for Children Under 13 ®
VIOLENCE, LANGUAGE, HORROR IMAGES, SLIME AND GORE

DOLBY

SOUNDTRACK AVAILABLE AT THE iTUNES MUSIC STORE | VARÈSE SARABANDE

www.avp-movie.com

An Anglo-Czech-Canadian-German Co-Production



20th Century Fox

LEVEL 2

SCHOLASTIC

**'Alien vs. Predator' adapted by:** Paul Shipton
**Commissioning Editor:** Jacquie Bloese
**Editor:** Clare Gray
**Designer:** Mo Choy
**Picture research:** Emma Bree
**Photo credits:**
Cover photo and inside photos courtesy of Fox.
**Page 46:** Allstar; AFP/Getty Images.
**Page 50:** Photodisc; A. Kowalski, M. Evans/Alamy.



Published by Scholastic Ltd. 2007



Mary Glasgow Magazines (Scholastic Ltd.)
Euston House
24 Eversholt Street
London
NW11DB

Printed in Singapore. Reprinted in 2009.
This edition printed in 2011.

# CONTENTS

# ALIEN VS.

### Charles Weyland

Weyland is a very rich man, but money is not enough for him. He wants the world to remember his name.

### Maxwell Stafford

Stafford has worked for Weyland for a long time. He is ready to do anything for his boss.

### Alexa (Lex) Woods

Lex Woods likes adventure. For her job, she takes people to dangerous places. Weyland needs her help.

### Adele Rousseau

Rousseau works for Weyland, too. She can fly a plane and she can use a gun.

## PLACES

### Bouvetoya Island

This small island of ice and snow is in the Antarctic Ocean. No one lives here and it is far away from any people or cities.

### The Piper Maru

Charles Weyland and his team travel to Bouvetoya Island on this ship. But will they ever see it again?

# PREDATOR

## Sebastian De Rosa

De Rosa has studied pyramids around the world for years. He has some very unusual ideas about them.

## Graham Miller

Miller loves his work – studying every-day things to discover new information. He always carries a camera.

## Mark Verheiden

Verheiden is a quiet man - but he is strong and very brave. He works for Weyland's company and Maxwell Stafford is his boss.

## Predators

They come from another world and they love to hunt and kill.

## Aliens

Young Aliens jump out of their eggs onto people's faces. Then they grow much bigger inside the person's body and jump out.

The Alien Queen has been asleep for a long time. Now she is awake, and she has an important job – making eggs ... LOTS of Alien eggs.

## The Pyramid

Far below the ice of Bouvetoya, there is a big pyramid. Is it the first pyramid in the world? Or does it hold a much bigger secret?

## The Predator Ship

It has travelled a long, long way across space to come to this world.

# ALIEN VS. PREDATOR

## CHAPTER 1

### Weyland's team

Far away, a satellite travelled through space. A camera on it took photos of our world, far below. It sent the information down to a station in Nebraska in the United States. This station was part of a big business called Weyland Industries.

Inside the station, a man was sitting in a room full of computers. He saw a red light on the computer in front of him and jumped up quickly.

'What is it?' asked one of the other workers.

'It's from Satellite 12,' he said. 'It's a heat photo of Area 14.'

The other worker did not understand. 'There isn't *anything* in Area 14,' she said.

The man's eyes did not move from the computer. 'There is now.'

***

Alexa Woods – Lex – was climbing an icy mountain in Nepal. She was alone, and the climb was difficult and dangerous. Lex loved it – she loved the cold and the snow. Most of all, she loved to test herself.

Suddenly there was a sound from her coat – Lex's mobile phone.

'Hello,' she said into the phone.

'Miss Woods,' answered a man's deep voice. 'I'm pleased to meet you.'

'Who is this?' asked Lex.

'My name is Maxwell Stafford. I work for Weyland Industries. Mr Weyland wants to meet you and offer you a job. He will pay a lot of money.'

Lex worked in the Antarctic. When anybody needed to go somewhere on the ice, she took them. She also worked to save animals in the area. She needed Weyland's money.

'When?' she asked.

'Tomorrow.'

'That's going to be a problem,' said Lex. 'It will take me a week to get back from here.'

As she spoke, Lex continued to climb. She was near the top of the mountain now. She pulled herself on to the top and looked up.

A tall man was looking down at her. There was a helicopter behind him. He spoke into his mobile phone.

'I told Mr Weyland that,' he said.

Lex looked at Stafford. 'What did he say?' she asked.

'We don't have a week.'

***

Mexico. Fifty kilometres from Mexico City. Hundreds of people were working in the hot sun near a big Aztec* pyramid. They were looking for old Aztec things. It was slow work in the Mexican heat.

Suddenly there were excited shouts. Something was happening – something big.

Workers ran to watch Professor Sebastian De Rosa. The Italian was looking into a hole at the bottom of an old Aztec wall.

'I think we are on top of it,' he said.

*The Aztec people lived in part of Mexico between the 1200s and the 1500s.

He was excited as he pushed his head and arms into the hole. It was deep and dark inside. He reached out and searched with his hand. It closed around something. But what? Something of the Aztecs? Something important? De Rosa had new ideas about old buildings like the pyramids. Now he was looking for proof.

'What is it, Sebastian?' asked Thomas, one of the other workers. 'What did you discover?'

De Rosa pulled himself out of the hole and stood up. He showed the thing in his hands. It wasn't Aztec; it was the top from a bottle of Pepsi!

De Rosa was angry and he could not hide it. But he did not lose all hope.

'We're going to find something here,' he told Thomas. 'I'll go to the bank in Mexico City and get us more money.'

'I can help with that,' said a deep voice. De Rosa looked up and saw a tall man. Maxwell Stafford.

He gave a letter to De Rosa. Inside it was money from Mr Weyland – a lot of money.

'We need some of your time,' explained Stafford.

***

A helicopter was flying over the dark, cold sea in the Antarctic. Lex Woods was sleeping inside the helicopter. She woke up and looked at the other passenger. He was a thin, Scottish man and he was trying to take a photo of himself.

'Did I wake you up? I'm sorry. I'm taking photos for my family,' he explained.

The man's name was Graham Miller. He looked excited to be there. 'Mr Weyland asked me to come and study something. I don't know what. Do *you* work for Mr Weyland?' he asked.

'No.' Lex smiled. 'I help people find places on the ice.' She looked out of the window.

The helicopter was moving towards a ship called the *Piper Maru* now. It was an ice breaker – a special kind of ship for the cold waters of the Antarctic.

But why were they flying towards it? What was waiting for them on the ship?

***

'Welcome,' said Maxwell Stafford. He was talking to about twenty people in a big room on the *Piper Maru*. Lex Woods and Graham Miller were there. Sebastian De Rosa was, too.

'You probably all have the same question – "why?" Why have we put this team together? Now you will find out the answer.' He looked up at the stairs above them. 'Mr Weyland …'

Everybody looked up. The owner of Weyland Industries stood at the top of the stairs.

'Seven days ago, one of my satellites over the Antarctic discovered something,' Weyland explained. 'Heat was coming from one area. We used it to make this computer map.'

Everybody looked up at a picture of a big building.

'The red lines are walls. The building is very big,' continued Weyland. 'It has got hundreds of rooms. My people tell me that it's a pyramid. But they can't agree about it. One of them says that it is like an Aztec pyramid. Another says that it is Cambodian*. And they all say that the sides of the pyramid are Egyptian*.'

'Your people are right,' said Sebastian De Rosa.

'Which one?'

'All of them,' answered the Italian. 'Perhaps this is the first pyramid ever.' He was on his feet, excited.

'But *who* built it?' asked Graham Miller.

'The first people,' said De Rosa. 'A long time ago, *before* the Egyptians, the Cambodians or the Aztecs, Antarctica had no ice. People lived here. Maybe these people were the first pyramid builders in the world!'

'Where is this place on the ice?' Lex asked Weyland.

'Bouvetoya Island,' he answered. 'But it's not *on* the ice. It's 600 metres *under* it.'

*Cambodia is a country in Southeast Asia. From the 800s to the 1300s, the Khmer Empire built many great buildings at the city of Angkor. The Egyptians first lived around the River Nile in North Africa about 5000 years ago. Their pyramids are probably the most famous in the world.

# CHAPTER 2

## Under the ice

'It will take seven days to get through the ice to the pyramid,' said a man called Quinn.

Lex spoke. 'We also need three weeks to train the team.'

'We don't have three weeks,' said Weyland. 'Other people will be here soon. I want to reach the pyramid first.'

But Lex continued. 'Nobody in this room is ready for Bouvetoya Island. If we find trouble, there's no help for thousands of kilometres.'

'It *is* dangerous,' agreed Weyland. 'But we can't say no to something like this.'

Weyland's words were true for everybody in the room ... except Lex.

'Find somebody else,' she said, and she walked to the door.

***

As Lex waited to fly home, she stood and watched the beautiful lights of the Antarctic in the dark sky. Graham Miller and Sebastian De Rosa joined her.

De Rosa looked worried. 'Let me ask you this,' he said to Lex. 'Will we do better *with* you or *without* you?'

A woman called Adele Rousseau joined them. 'Miss Woods, your helicopter is ready.'

But Lex was thinking. Could she leave the others here? She knew the answer – no.

***

Something was moving through the dark of space. Something big – much bigger than a satellite. It was a spaceship, and it was not from this world. It came closer.

Suddenly a blue light shot out of the ship. It flew straight towards the Antarctic ... and Bouvetoya Island.

***

Weyland's team was almost ready to leave the *Piper Maru* and go across the ice to the pyramid.

'Everybody listen!' shouted Lex. 'My job is to keep you all safe, and you can help me. Never go anywhere alone. Be ready – bad things can happen on the ice.'

The team continued to get ready. Adele Rousseau had a gun in her hands.

'Guns aren't very useful on the ice,' Lex told her. 'Why are you bringing it?'

'I like to be ready,' answered Adele, 'for anything.' She smiled at Lex. 'I'm happy that you're coming with us.'

At last it was time to leave. The team went out on to the ice. It was a long way to Bouvetoya Island ...

***

They arrived a few hours later. Lex shot a flare into the night sky. By its light everyone looked down on an old fishing station.

'It's empty,' explained Lex. 'People last used it in 1904. But then everybody just disappeared. Nobody knows why.' She looked at Weyland. 'The pyramid is right under it.'

When they got to the station, Quinn and his men started work. They needed to put together their ice-cutting machines. They wanted to reach the pyramid as soon as possible. The rest of the team began to look around the old station. Suddenly there was a shout from De Rosa.

'Over here!' he called to the others.

He was standing next to a big hole in the ice. The hole looked deep. They lit a flare and dropped it in. It went down and down.

'How far does it go?' asked Lex.

Weyland looked at his computer. 'All the way down to the pyramid,' he said. 'But yesterday this hole wasn't here.'

'Then why is it here now?' asked Miller uncertainly.

Quinn had no answers. 'Nothing in the world can make a hole so deep in twenty-four hours,' he said.

But the hole was not going to stop Weyland. 'We'll find the answers when we get down there,' he said.

***

The Predators looked down at the Antarctic from their ship in space. They were not from this world, but they knew this place.

Three of them got their weapons and put on their helmets. It was almost time to leave the ship.

***

Quinn and his men worked fast because a storm was coming. While the rest of the team waited, Lex found Weyland. The rich man looked bad. His face was white.

'You can't go down to the pyramid if you're ill,' said Lex. 'It's too dangerous. Stay on the ship.'

'When you're ill, you start to think about your life,' said Weyland. 'How will people remember you? I hope that people will remember me for this.'

Lex understood. Her father was just like Weyland.

'I need this,' said Weyland.

***

At last it was time. The team started the long climb down to the pyramid. Lex went into the dark ice tunnel first and the others followed. Everybody held the long ropes and went down carefully.

Outside the tunnel, the storm reached Bouvetoya Island. The wind was very strong. Wind and snow hit Quinn and his men in the face as they worked. It was too dangerous to be outside in this storm. Quinn started to run towards a building.

'Quick!' he shouted to his men.

It was hard to see through the heavy snow… hard to hear anything except the noise of the wind. Quinn did not see or hear the spaceship as it flew over his head.

The spaceship flew quietly past the station. Then it shot three little ships out. These flew down and landed in the ice. They started to open. The Predators were here …

## CHAPTER 3

### The hunt starts

The team reached the end of the tunnel at last, far under the station.

Lex lit another flare and looked around.

'I don't understand it,' said Weyland. 'There's nothing here. No sign of another team.'

'Somebody made that tunnel,' said Lex.

One of the team turned on a big light and everyone became quiet. They couldn't believe their eyes. Here, far under the ice of the Antarctic, they were looking at a big pyramid.

'You did it, Mr Weyland,' said Lex softly. 'People *will* remember you for this …'

Weyland spoke to everybody. 'Thank you,' he said. 'Thank you all for this. Let's go.'

They started to walk towards the pyramid's entrance. It was dark inside. The tall walls had strange writing and pictures all over them. One picture showed a fight between two strange animals.

Sebastian De Rosa studied the writing on the walls. Some letters looked like Aztec writing and some looked like Cambodian. That meant just one thing – De Rosa's ideas about the first pyramids were right!

***

Weyland's team didn't know it, but the pyramid was like a machine. It was waiting for someone to turn it on. When the team went through the entrance, they did this – they turned it on. Now, in a different part of the pyramid, the floor started to move. Slowly something started coming up into the room from under the floor. Long, thick chains pulled it up – a living thing. But it wasn't something from our world. This terrible black thing was like something from your worst dreams – an Alien!

There was ice all over the Alien, but it was not dead. It was waking up now after a long, long sleep. It moved slowly at first, then faster. It could not move much because strong chains held its arms and legs. It looked around and gave a shout – a shout of complete hate at everything around it.

This was the Alien Queen and she had a special job to do – make eggs. Lots and lots of Alien eggs.

***

Quinn's men waited and listened to the storm outside. But suddenly they heard something else above the sound of the wind – a cry, and then a different sound – something strange.

Suddenly the door opened and something came in. The men couldn't really see it – it almost looked like clear water. But then a cold knife pushed right through one of the men. Its end was red with the man's blood.

Then something threw another man across the room.

The frightened men started to fire their guns, but it was hard with nothing to shoot *at*. Something pushed one man back against the wall, hard. He cried out. He was dying, but how? Something was in him – cold and hard. He couldn't see anything but he could *feel* it with his hands. When he looked down, a long spear slowly started to appear. He didn't understand; there was no time to understand, because then everything went black.

***

Quinn was at the top of the tunnel when he heard strange sounds. Something was wrong! He was the boss up here; he had to find out. He ran to one of the buildings. But when he opened the door, he saw something terrible. It was a man – one of *his* men – and he was dead. Quinn didn't see anyone else in the room, but *something* was pulling the dead man up by a rope around his legs. The man was hanging down like a piece of meat.

Suddenly a spear flew out at Quinn. It didn't hit him, and he didn't wait for another. He turned and ran through the snow. He didn't understand, but he knew one thing – he had to escape.

But there was no escape. In the next building, Quinn found more dead men. These were hanging by their feet, too. Who killed them?

Quinn took a gun in his hands. Outside, he saw something on top of the building – again it was hard to see; it looked like water, like a ghost. Quinn fired his gun at the thing, but it was no good.

The thing on the roof was a Predator. Guns were nothing to it. Quinn could not really see it because it was using a special machine. With the machine, nobody – and nothing – could see the Predator during a hunt. The Predator turned the machine off now.

Quinn watched as the Predator jumped down off the building. He tried to fight, but the Predator was bigger and stronger.

It hit the man away easily. Quinn fell back into the tunnel, all the way down to the pyramid.

The Predator watched him fall. Two others joined it and all three Predators looked down into the dark. It was time – time for them to go to the pyramid.

***

Inside the pyramid, Weyland's team stood in a big, round room with seven tables. On each table there was a dead body. These looked hundreds of years old.

'What is all this?' Weyland asked quietly.

'Their own people killed them,' said De Rosa, looking at the old, black bodies. 'The Aztecs and the Egyptians did the same thing in their pyramids.' He studied one of the bodies. 'No ropes or chains tied these people down. They *chose* to die.' He started to read the words on the table. '*When they gave their lives, the hunt could start,*' he read.

Adele Rousseau was looking at the hole in one of the dead bodies. 'This is unusual,' she said. 'I think something broke *out* of this body.'

***

Quinn was not dead after his fall, but he could not move. He could not do anything as the first two Predators walked past him towards the pyramid. They did not even look at him. Were they going to just leave him here?

But then he heard the sound of a knife. Quinn turned his head and saw the third Predator above him. It was the last thing he ever saw.

## CHAPTER 4

### No escape in the dark

Inside the pyramid, Maxwell Stafford found a tunnel down to another part of the building.

'Let's go,' said Weyland.

'We're moving to the next room,' Stafford told the others. He told Thomas and Adele to stay in the room with the seven tables.

The rest of the team continued through the dark tunnels of the pyramid. When they reached the next room, they found another big table. De Rosa studied the words on top of it.

'It shows dates,' he said and he pointed to different words. 'These are days, these are months, and here are the years.' His hand rested on a round part of the table top. 'And *this* is some kind of lock.' He studied it some more. 'Somebody last opened this in … 1904.' He looked up. 'What's today's date?'

Lex told him, and the Italian started to turn parts of the table top. When all the dates were in the right place, suddenly there was a sound. The table started to move and open.

'Have a look at this,' said De Rosa.

There were three things inside the table. They looked like weapons – guns of some kind – but not usual guns. The team did not know what they were. But they knew one thing – they were very important.

Lex was thinking about other things – Mr Weyland was looking tired and ill again.

'That's enough for today,' she told the team. 'We can stay at the fishing station tonight, then start again here tomorrow.'

Stafford pointed at the three strange weapons. 'What do

you want to do with these things, Mr Weyland?'

'Take them,' said the rich man. 'We'll do more tests on them at the station.'

Stafford's men reached in to take the three things.

'No!' cried De Rosa, but he was too late. Weyland's men took the strange weapons in their hands. Then, all at once, the room changed around them. The table closed; the door closed, too. On the other side of the room, a new door appeared with stairs down into another part of the pyramid.

***

In the room with the seven tables, the doors started to close, too. Adele tried to push something under one of them, but it was no good. There was no way out.

Suddenly there was another noise. A hole appeared in each of the tables. Something came up through each hole – Alien eggs!

Adele's gun was in her hands. She and Thomas watched as the eggs opened with a wet sound.

Suddenly thin legs appeared at the top of each egg. These were the Alien Queen's eggs, and the things inside them were new Aliens.

Thomas and Adele were frightened, but there was nowhere to go. Suddenly the young Aliens used their long tails to jump. There were too many of them to shoot. Before Adele could fire her gun, one of the Aliens was on her face. Its thin, strong legs were around her head. Then Adele's world turned black.

***

In the other room, the team heard the gun and Adele's terrible cries.

'Adele!' Stafford shouted into his radio. 'Can you hear me?'

No answer.

'What *is* this place?' Lex asked Weyland angrily.

'I don't know.'

'We're going to get everybody together and go back up to the station,' said Lex. 'Let's move!'

***

Adele Rousseau woke up. The body of the Alien thing lay next to her on its back. Was it dead? It wasn't moving.

Adele sat up and looked around. There was another Alien on Thomas' face. Its long tail went around his neck.

Suddenly Adele cried out. She could feel something. There was something *inside* her and it was moving. It was trying to get out!

Suddenly there was blood everywhere – Adele's blood. Then the head of an Alien appeared. It was different now – bigger and stronger.

The Alien gave a terrible cry, but Adele Rousseau could not hear this. She was dead.

***

They didn't know it, but something was watching Lex, Weyland and the others – a Predator. It didn't have a light but it didn't need one. Its helmet allowed it to see things in the dark by their heat. It could see them clearly – and it could see the three special guns in their bag. Predator guns!

'Let's keep moving,' shouted Lex. 'We're close to the entrance.' They were in a long tunnel.

Suddenly the Predator threw its spear down. It hit and killed one of Weyland's men. Some of the team tried to hide. Stafford and his men started to fire their guns, but they couldn't see the Predator.

And then the pyramid started moving again all around them. Walls moved, parts of the floor moved; doors closed and new ones appeared. It all happened very quickly.

'The pyramid is changing again!' shouted Miller.

Lex pulled Weyland through one door before it closed. De Rosa and Stafford followed them.

Graham Miller and Verheiden, one of Stafford's men, were too slow. As the walls moved around them, they looked for another way out. There wasn't one.

# CHAPTER 5

## Predators' blood

In another room, Lex and the others had the same problem – they couldn't go anywhere either.

'Just wait,' said De Rosa.

'Why?' asked Lex.

De Rosa looked at his watch. 'I think the pyramid moves every ten minutes,' he said.

He was right – after ten minutes the walls moved again and there was another door in front of them.

***

The same thing happened in Verheiden and Miller's room. The two men shone their lights into a new tunnel ahead. Miller went first with the light, and Verheiden followed with his gun.

Verheiden heard a sound. He stopped. It sounded like something living, but what? He looked around. Where was it coming from?

Suddenly a hole appeared below Verheiden. He fell down into it.

'Get me out of here!' called Verheiden.

But there was no time – the hole down to the tunnel below was already closing. Miller couldn't do anything to stop it.

'No!' cried Verheiden. He didn't want to be alone in this tunnel. But then he looked up and saw that he *wasn't* alone. Something was moving at the other end of the tunnel.

It came out of the dark and Verheiden was looking into the terrible face of an Alien. Verheiden took his gun in his hands. 'Come on then!' he shouted angrily.

Before he fired, there was another sound from behind him, even closer. Another Alien! It was the end for Verheiden.

In the tunnel above, Graham Miller could hear Verheiden's cries, but he couldn't do anything to help. Then he heard another sound. He looked up and all thoughts of Verheiden disappeared.

The Aliens were coming for Miller, too …

***

'Weyland, are you OK?' asked Lex.

It was more and more difficult for the ill man to continue. He needed to rest. He dropped the Predator's gun.

'Leave it,' said Lex. 'It will only make us slower.'

'We've lost too much already,' said Weyland. 'We can't leave with nothing.'

'Give it to me.' Lex put the gun into the bag on her back.

Stafford was at the front of the group now. Suddenly some ropes shot out at him. He fired his gun, but it was no good. The ropes were over him – he could not move.

The others ran to help him, but even De Rosa's big knife could not cut the ropes.

'Look out!' shouted Stafford.

A Predator was coming towards them! Lex ran at it, but it hit her away easily. Then it lifted De Rosa with one big hand.

With the other hand it pointed its long spear at Stafford. The spear shot out and then Maxwell Stafford was dead, too.

There was no time for Lex to worry about Weyland's man. She had to help De Rosa.

The Predator still held the Italian and soon he was going to die. Lex reached for a gun, but something hit her hard.

It was a second Predator, but this one was using its special machine. She could not really see it clearly. But she could see the knife. It appeared suddenly and Lex understood – this was the end.

No! Suddenly something else moved behind the Predator – something big. A long tail moved easily through the Predator's body. It lifted the dying Predator up off the floor.

Lex could see the Predator now, and she could see the terrible thing behind it – an Alien! It put its face close to the Predator's helmet. Its mouth opened and a second mouth shot out. Green blood fell as the Predator died.

The Predator with De Rosa turned. He threw the man down and ran to fight the Alien. The Predator had to keep away from the Alien's teeth and its tail.

Lex ran to De Rosa. 'We have to get Weyland,' she told him. They helped Weyland up and started running. Behind them, the fight between Predator and Alien continued.

The Alien's tail went around the Predator's feet and pulled it down to the floor. Then it jumped on top of the Predator, ready to kill. But the Predator moved too quickly. It turned around and cut off the end of the Alien's tail with its knife.

The Predator was on its feet and running now. It pushed the Alien back, and took its tail in its hands. Then it threw the Alien across the room.

The Predator ran. But, in a moment, the Alien was jumping down at the Predator. The Predator shot more ropes out. The ropes caught the Alien, but not for long. The next moment, the Alien was free. It pushed the Predator down and opened its mouth. More green Predator blood fell.

The second Predator was dead. Now there was only one inside the pyramid. But where?

***

Lex and De Rosa were almost carrying Weyland now as they ran for the entrance.

'What *were* those things?' asked De Rosa.

'You tell me,' said Lex. 'You know about pyramids!'

Weyland could not continue. 'I've got to stop,' he said. He sat down on the stairs and rested.

Suddenly something appeared at the other end of the room – the last Predator!

'There's another one!' cried De Rosa. 'We have to go!'

Lex tried to help Weyland up, but he spoke to De Rosa. 'Sebastian, get her out of here now! Run!'

De Rosa pulled Lex away towards the door, as Weyland stood. The Predator pushed him to the floor easily. An ill man like Weyland was no danger. The Predator moved to the stairs.

'Don't turn your back on me!' shouted Weyland. He pulled out a flare and lit it. He held it in his hand as the fire shot out at the Predator.

The Predator stopped. It turned, its knife ready. It pushed the knife into Weyland and the rich man fell back, dead.

Weyland's dream was over.

# CHAPTER 6

## The first visit

The Predator was coming for them. Lex and De Rosa knew that. And they couldn't do anything to stop it.

But then suddenly walls started to move. The pyramid was changing again.

'This way!' shouted De Rosa.

They ran and jumped quickly into a tunnel. It was the only way out now! The tunnel was very small – and it was getting smaller! They had to lie down and pull themselves through it. Just in time, they pulled themselves into the next room. The tunnel closed behind them.

***

The Predator waited on the other side of the wall.

But it was not alone. One of the young Aliens from the eggs jumped out at it. Quickly the Predator pulled out a knife and threw it. Before the Alien landed on the Predator's face, the knife hit it. A moment later, the Alien was on the floor in two halves.

That was the easy part. But there was also a big Alien in the room. Did the Predator know about it? The Alien started to climb slowly down the wall, closer and closer … Suddenly the Predator turned. The knife was still in its hand, the Predator moved like the wind, and then … the big Alien's head fell to the floor, too. Its dead body followed.

***

In the other room, Lex found a small hole in the wall. It was much too small to climb into, but she could look through at the room behind them. She could see the

Predator. It was taking its helmet off.

'Look over here,' Lex told De Rosa.

They watched as the Predator broke off part of the dead Alien's hand. Carefully, it used the Alien's finger to put a sign on its helmet. Smoke came off the helmet as the Alien's skin touched it. Next, the Predator used the Alien's finger to put a sign on its own face.

'It's giving itself a sign of the hunt,' explained De Rosa quietly. 'A long time ago many hunters did the same thing. They killed something and then put a sign on themselves with blood from the dead body.'

He turned to Lex. 'I'm starting to understand all of this,' he said. He pointed to the writing on the wall. 'It's not easy to read, but the story is all here,' explained De Rosa. 'These hunters came to our world a long time ago. They taught people how to build – they made great pyramids across the world.

'Every hundred years, the hunters returned. They came back to hunt the most dangerous thing ever – Aliens. They let these Aliens grow inside the people of our world. Then the hunters fought these terrible Aliens. When a hunter killed one, it could wear the sign of the hunter on its face. It was proof of the fight. But the hunters did not always win. When this happened, they did not let the Aliens live. They used a bomb to kill everything and everybody in the area.'

Lex was trying to understand. 'So the hunters brought those Aliens here to our world?' she asked. 'To hunt them?'

'Yes. And the Aliens grew *inside* us. Without us, there was no hunt.'

***

Graham Miller's eyes opened. He could not move. There was something hard and black all over his body. Only his head and one arm were free. He looked to the side. Verheiden was next to him, but there was one of the little Aliens right on his face. Its thin, strong legs held Verheiden's head.

There was a wet noise in front of Miller. He looked down and saw one of the Alien eggs. It was opening, and something began to move inside.

Miller was more frightened than ever, but then he saw something – Verheiden's gun. Miller *had* to reach that gun. It was very difficult even to move his arm, but he tried his hardest. The little Alien was out of the egg now; it was getting ready to jump …

At last Miller got the gun! As the little Alien flew towards his face, Miller pointed and fired. The Alien fell to the floor in a shower of green blood. Miller fired at it again and again.

And then he looked up. The room was *full* of eggs, lots and lots of them.

And they were all opening …

***

Sebastian De Rosa looked at the door between them and the Predator. 'When that door opens, we're dead.'

'Not if we make things right,' said Lex quietly. 'The hunters made this pyramid to keep the Aliens in. But we took the hunters' guns, and now the Aliens are running free. The hunters *need* their guns … When that door opens, we're going to give the hunter his gun back.'

'It will kill us!' said De Rosa.

'No, they're not hunting us! We need to choose a side in this fight.' Her eyes met De Rosa's. 'If those Alien things reach our world, everything everywhere dies!'

Sounds started all around them – the pyramid was moving again. Another door opened in front of them.

'Let's find our friend,' said Lex.

***

They were walking down another long, dark tunnel when they heard new sounds. Was it the Predator? No, this sounded different.

And then they saw it – it wasn't the Predator. It was an Alien!

There was nothing to do except turn and run. They ran through the tunnel as fast as they could. But ahead of them there was a big, deep hole in the floor. De Rosa did not slow down. He jumped right across the hole. Lex tried to do the same, but she couldn't reach the far side. She fell but her hands caught the edge. She was hanging by her hands.

De Rosa ran to help her. His hand reached hers just as she began to fall.

'Come on, Lex!' he shouted, as he started to pull her up.

She was almost safe. But when she looked up, she didn't only see De Rosa. The Alien was behind him!

'No!' cried Lex.

But the Alien pulled Sebastian De Rosa away.

Now Lex was alone.

# CHAPTER 7

## Friends

When Lex pulled herself up in the room, it was empty and quiet. There was no Alien, and no De Rosa.

Lex continued alone through empty tunnels. In the next room she looked for another door. She was tired and frightened. She was losing hope now. She looked around, and saw the Predator.

It was standing there quietly. Its spear was in its hand – it was time to kill again.

'Wait!' cried Lex. She lifted her empty hands. 'Please wait!' Slowly she took the bag off her back and threw it to the Predator – the gun!

But there was no time for the Predator to get it. Another Alien was behind it! It turned and started to fight. The spear fell to the floor, but the Predator threw the Alien to one side. When it got up, Lex was in front of it. It jumped at her.

Just in time, Lex got the Predator's spear from the floor. The Alien looked at her. It was moving closer to her now.

She lifted the spear and it went right through the Alien's body. It took a long time to die. It tried to reach Lex with its teeth and with its tail, but Lex's hands did not leave the spear. At last, the Alien died.

Lex looked across the room. The Predator had its gun now. Was it going to shoot her? No, it turned quickly – more Aliens were coming into the room. The Predator shot and killed one, then another.

The Aliens were not going to stop. They did not care about guns. But then they heard a cry from another part of the pyramid. It was the Alien Queen and it was calling to them all. The Aliens ran back into the dark.

***

The Predator got its spear and started to go to the door.

'Wait!' shouted Lex. 'I'm coming with you. Do you hear me?'

The Predator turned quickly. It could kill Lex easily; she knew that. But the Predator did not kill her. With its knife it took off the dead Alien's tail.

'What are you doing?' asked Lex.

Then Lex understood. The Predator was making a weapon for her. The Alien's tail was a spear! Now she was ready to fight.

***

The Aliens came to their mother, the Alien Queen. Chains still held her, but now it was time to lose them. The Aliens jumped up and started to break the chains. Soon the biggest, most dangerous Alien of all was going to be free.

***

Lex saw something on the floor in the next tunnel – a camera.

'Miller?' she shouted.

She went into the room and saw all the Alien eggs. Then she saw Miller and Verheiden. The two men were not moving.

Lex went further into the room and found De Rosa. Like Miller, the Italian could not move – something hard and black covered his body.

But De Rosa was not sleeping. He turned his frightened eyes towards Lex.

'Help me!' he called. 'The thing is inside me. Lex, these terrible things must not get out of the pyramid!'

Lex understood. She lifted Verheiden's gun with both hands and pointed it at De Rosa. It was a difficult job, but it was the only way to help De Rosa now.

'I'm sorry,' said Lex. And then she fired.

The Predator just watched as Lex dropped the gun and turned away. Moments later, the little Alien jumped out of De Rosa's dead body. The Predator caught it easily in one hand and killed it.

The Predator looked back at the eggs in the room. Each one of them had an Alien in it. The eggs started to open. The Predator took a machine from its arm and turned it on. He threw it to the floor.

Lex watched this and understood. 'It's a bomb,' she said. 'I hope it kills all of them!'

Now they started to run through the tunnel to the entrance of the pyramid. Lex and the Predator kept on running – down the main stairs, and back to the tunnel. A sled was waiting for them there. Lex and the Predator jumped quickly on to the sled and rode back up the tunnel to the station.

***

Back in the pyramid, there was a terrible sound – the Predator's bomb! A big ball of fire shot out. No more eggs, no more Aliens … No more pyramid! The fire followed Lex and the Predator up the tunnel too, but they reached the top just in time. At last – they were safe!

The Predator turned to Lex. Slowly he reached one hand up to his helmet and took it off. Lex looked up into the face of something from another world.

The Predator still had a part of an Alien's hand. He moved it towards Lex and put the sign of the hunter on Lex's face.

Suddenly there was a terrible sound behind them. Something big broke out of the ice. It was the Alien Queen! Chains still hung from her arms and legs, but she was free. All her children were dead – and she was angry!

The Predator threw a spear at her, then a knife. But the Alien Queen was too strong. She hit the Predator with her tail and the Predator fell to the ice. Lex ran at the Alien Queen and pushed her own spear into the Alien Queen's body. There was green blood everywhere. The Alien

Queen fell back into one of the buildings. But she was not dead, and now Lex had no weapons. She ran.

The Alien Queen followed. With her long legs, she was much faster. Lex tried to hide inside one of the buildings, but it didn't help. Soon the Alien Queen was going to kill her.

Suddenly something jumped up high above the Alien Queen. It was the Predator! It pushed its spear into the Alien Queen's head.

Lex ran out of the building. It was near the edge of the ice and soon it was going to fall into the cold water. The Queen still wasn't dead. But suddenly Lex had an idea. She looked at one of the chains around the Queen's arms. Quickly she started to pull the other end of the chain. She was trying to get it around part of the building. The Predator saw her and started to help.

'I've got it!' shouted Lex. The chain was on!

Now they had to wait for the building to fall. But it was too late for the Predator. The end of the Alien Queen's tail pushed through the Predator's body and lifted it up. At last the building fell, down into the dark, cold waters below. The Queen's tail threw the Predator to one side. But the Queen could not escape because of the chain. The building pulled her into the icy waters with it, far down into the cold and the dark.

Lex went to the Predator. She had no words. But she sat with the great hunter as it died in the snow.

Suddenly there was a light behind her. A spaceship appeared above her. A new Predator was standing in front of her. It looked older. It saw the sign of the hunter on Lex's face and understood. While others carried the dead Predator back to the ship, this old one lifted a spear. It held the spear out to Lex. This weapon was hers now.

And then the Predators were back in their ship, and it flew up into the dark sky. Lex stood alone in the night and watched it go.

***

The Predator ship was leaving this world. They were going home. The body of the dead Predator lay on a table. Everything was quiet. But then suddenly something moved – something *inside* the Predator's body. A shower of green blood shot up, and then something came out …

A *new* kind of life. Half Alien, half Predator – and more terrible than either …

# THE FILM

The 2004 film *Alien vs. Predator*, or *AVP*, brings two very popular film series together – the Alien films and the Predator films.

## Alien

Sigourney Weaver in *Alien*

The first Alien film appeared in 1979. Its story happens 150 years in the future. A terrible alien comes on to a spaceship and kills the people one by one. Only a woman called Ripley (actor Sigourney Weaver) can stop it.

The film was very popular all around the world. Later, there were three more films in the series, all with Sigourney Weaver.

## Predator

*Predator* was first in cinemas in 1987. This story is about a special kind of alien – a Predator! Everything happens here on Earth in the present day. A Predator hunts a group of people – but then it tries to kill Arnold Schwarzenegger. Big mistake!

A second film in the series moved the Predators to a big city.

A Predator in *Predator 2*

**Have you seen any of the Alien or Predator films? Which one(s)? Why are they popular, do you think?**

# Alien meets Predator!

Aliens and Predators met for the first time in a 1989 comic book from Dark Horse Comics. Film-makers were soon excited about the idea of a film with the two aliens!

There were lots of ideas for the story, and all of them happened in space. But British director Paul W. S. Anderson wanted the film to be on Earth.

The story of *AVP* happens *after* the Predator films and *before* the Alien films.

Sanaa Lathan as Lex Woods

# The actors

Director Paul Anderson wanted a strong woman in the story, just like the Alien films. The film-makers chose African-American **Sanaa Lathan** to play Lex Woods.

Actor **Lance Henrikson** plays Charles Bishop Weyland, the head of a big company. The same actor played Bishop, a human-looking robot in the second Alien film, *Aliens*. He also played Bishop II in *Alien*$^3$.

**Arnold Schwarzenegger**, the star of the first Predator film, did not appear in *AVP*. But he *almost* did! Film-makers spoke to him about appearing at the end of the film. Schwarzenegger was interested – but then he became the Governor of California. He was too busy with his new job, so the film-makers dropped this idea.

**Do you know what these words mean? You can use a dictionary.**
**series actor director robot Governor**

# MAKING

In a film like *AVP*, special effects are very important. Unlike many directors today, Paul Anderson likes to use models as much as possible. He thinks that these effects often look better than computer special effects.

## AVP special effects

*AVP*'s special effects people worked hard on the Aliens and Predators to make them look 'real'. Predators look more like people than Aliens, so it was easy to use actors in special Predator suits for their scenes.

A fight between a Predator and an Alien in *AVP*.

Making the Aliens was more difficult. Sometimes they used people in suits, but more often they used models. The Alien Queen model was very, very big. Computers remembered its moves and the film-makers chose the best ones for the film. Sometimes the film-makers made pictures of the Aliens with computers – for example, when we can see hundreds of Aliens on the pyramid.

It was a hard job to bring the Aliens and Predators together. The film's first big fight between a Predator and an Alien took one month to film!

**What kind of film uses lots of special effects? Do you like this sort of film? Why/why not?**

AVP

## Who are the Predators?

Just one man – British actor Ian Whyte – played all the main Predators in the film. At over two metres tall (he was once a basketball player) he was just right for the job!

For some parts of the film, Whyte wore a special Predator's face, too. The film-makers used radio controls to move and change this face.

## Life cycle of an Alien

*AVP* special effects workers made different Alien models for each part of an Alien's life:

**First, the Alien Queen makes lots of eggs.**

**Then the little Aliens jump out of the eggs on to people's faces.**

**Next, the Aliens grow inside people's bodies. At last, they jump out of the bodies – ready to fight!**

**Do you know what these words mean? You can use a dictionary.**
**special effects director model suit scene control life cycle**

FACT FILE

# PYRAMIDS

**In *AVP*, Sebastian De Rosa studies pyramids from very different places and times – Egyptian, Cambodian and Aztec.**

## Ancient Egypt (3150 – 31BC)

**Ancient pyramids at Giza**

The Ancient Egyptian empire first grew around the river Nile in North Africa almost 5000 years ago. The Egyptians put the bodies of their dead kings deep inside their pyramids. They thought that the king could climb up and join the sun god in the sky.

The Great Pyramid of Giza, near Cairo, is one of the most famous buildings in the world. It took about 2,300,000 big stones to make it!

## The Khmer Empire (802 – 1327)

Angkor, in present day Cambodia, was the most important city in the Khmer empire. At one time, it was the biggest city in the world.

Much of the city is still there – including its famous temple, Angkor Wat. This wonderful ancient temple is the biggest religious building ever, with walls 800m long. One million people visit Angkor every year.

**Angkor Wat**

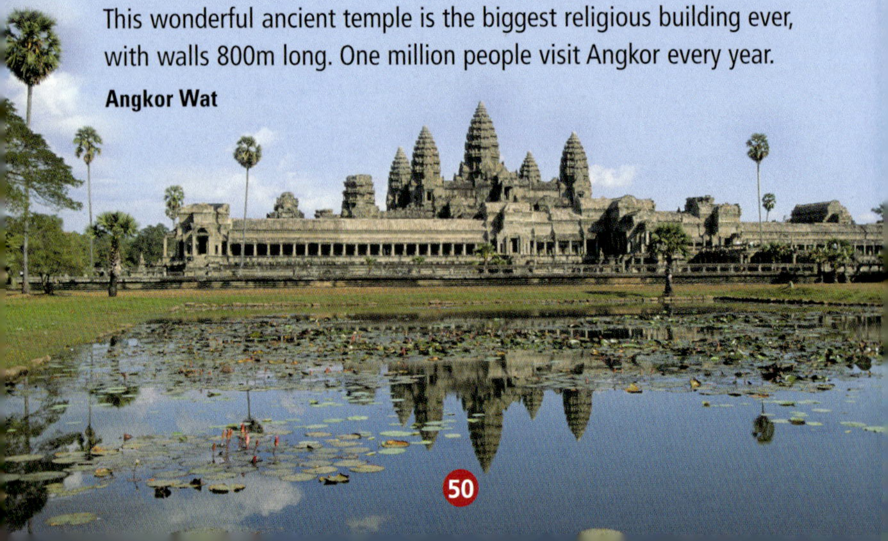

# AROUND THE WORLD

## The Aztecs (1248 – 1521)

The Aztec people lived in central Mexico long before any Spanish people arrived there. Their main city, Tenochititlan, is now Mexico City. The biggest building in the city was the Great Pyramid. Sometimes the Aztecs killed people here and offered them to their gods!

**The Great Pyramid at Tenochititlan**

The Aztec empire ended soon after Hernán Cortés and his Spanish men arrived in Mexico in 1519.

**Are there any famous ancient buildings in your country? What do you know about them? Have you visited any of them?**

## The first pyramid?

In the 1970s, the ideas of Erich von Daniken, a Swiss writer, became quite popular for a while. He believed that aliens helped people to build the world's pyramids!

In *AVP*, De Rosa's ideas are almost the same. He thinks that the pyramid under Bouvetoya Island may be the world's first pyramid. He believes that aliens helped men to build it a long, long time ago. It's a great idea for the film, but most people don't agree with von Daniken these days!

**Do you know what these words mean? You can use a dictionary.**

**ancient empire god temple religious**

# CHAPTERS 1–2

## Before you read

You can use a dictionary for this section.

**1** Use these words to complete the sentences.

**flare helmet rope weapon**

**a)** It was dark and so he lit a … .
**b)** A gun is a dangerous … .
**c)** They threw the … around the horse.
**d)** Put a … on your head.

**2** Use these words to answer the questions.

**alien ice satellite space**

**a)** Where are the stars?
**b)** What is hard and cold?
**c)** What flies in space?
**d)** What does not come from this world?

**3** Match the two columns.

| | | | |
|---|---|---|---|
| **a)** | The **helicopter** got them | **i)** | eats birds and mice. |
| **b)** | A computer is a very | **ii)** | down from the mountain. |
| **c)** | It's dangerous to | **iii)** | **shoot** a gun. |
| **d)** | A cat is a **predator** that | **iv)** | useful **machine**. |

**4** Which is which?

**pyramid tunnel**

**a)** A train goes under the mountain in a … .
**b)** A … is an old building.

**5** Look at 'People and Places' on pages 4–5.

**a)** Which people are going to die in this story, do you think?
**b)** Which people are going to live?

## After you read

**6** Answer these questions.

**a)** What does the satellite find in the Antarctic?
**b)** Where does Maxwell Stafford find Lex Woods?
**c)** What does Professor Sebastian De Rosa find in Mexico?

d) Where does Charles Weyland's team first meet?
e) What is far under the ice at Bouvetoya Island?
f) What comes to Bouvetoya Island from space?

7 Complete the sentences with the correct names.
**Sebastian De Rosa   Charles Weyland   Predators**
**Graham Miller   Adele Rousseau   Lex Woods**
a) ... often works in the Antarctic.
b) ... knows about pyramids.
c) ... takes photographs for his family.
d) ... has brought a gun with her.
e) ... wants the world to know his name.
f) ... are not from this world.

8 Are these sentences true or false?
a) Mr. Weyland is a poor man.
b) De Rosa thinks that the first people built the pyramid.
c) Lex is excited about going to the pyramid.
d) The pyramid is under an old fishing station.
e) Quinn does not hear the spaceship because the ice-cutting machines are very loud.

9 What do you think?
a) At the end of Chapter 2, Predators land on the island. What will they do next?
b) What will the team find in the pyramid?

## CHAPTERS 3-5

### Before you read

You can use a dictionary for this section.

10 Use these words to complete these sentences.
**chain   hunt   spear   tails**
a) Horses have very long ... .
b) People use guns to ... .
c) The ... on my bicycle broke.
d) He threw the ... a long way.

**After you read**

**11** Put these parts of the story in the correct order.

**a)** The team find three special guns.
**b)** The team go inside the pyramid.
**c)** Something kills Quinn's men.
**d)** The team find seven old bodies on tables.
**e)** The walls of the pyramid start to move.
**f)** The Alien Queen wakes up.
**g)** A Predator kills Mr Weyland.
**h)** Alien eggs come up through the holes in the seven tables.

**12** Match the two columns

| | |
|---|---|
| **a)** Thomas ... | **i)** has an alien inside her. |
| **b)** Mr Weyland ... | **ii)** has a long tail and two mouths. |
| **c)** The Alien ... | **iii)** has an alien on his face. |
| **d)** The Predators... | **iv)** is very ill. |
| **e)** Verheiden ... | **v)** falls into a big hole. |
| **f)** Adele ... | **vi)** have machines that stop anybody from seeing them. |

**13** Are these sentences true or false?

**a)** Quinn kills an alien.
**b)** Only one Predator goes into the Pyramid.
**c)** De Rosa does not want Stafford to take the three weapons.
**d)** Two Predators die.
**e)** Lex, Weyland and De Rosa try to leave the pyramid.
**f)** A Predator kills Charles Weyland.

## CHAPTERS 6–7

**Before you read**

You can use a dictionary for this section.

**14** Which is which?

**bomb** **sled**

**a)** A ... is very dangerous.
**b)** A ... goes fast down a snowy mountain.

**15** What do you think?

**a)** Lex and De Rosa are trying to escape. Will they both escape?

**b)** Why have the Predators come to Bouvetoya Island?

Now read Chapters 6–7 to see if you are right.

**After you read**

**16** Put these sentences in order.

**a)** The last Predator makes a weapon for Lex.

**b)** Lex gives one of the three special guns to the Predator.

**c)** Another Predator ship comes to our world.

**d)** Lex spears the Alien Queen but she doesn't die.

**e)** The Predator kills a little Alien and cuts another Alien's head off.

**f)** The Aliens break the Queen's chains.

**g)** Sebastian De Rosa dies.

**h)** The Alien Queen falls into the water and dies.

**17** Are these sentences true or false?

**a)** The Predator puts a sign on his helmet.

**b)** Graham Miller uses a gun to escape from the Aliens.

**c)** The Aliens come every hundred years to hunt.

**d)** The Predators brought the Aliens to our world.

**e)** The Alien Queen isn't strong.

**f)** De Rosa shoots Lex.

**g)** Lex sits with the Predator as it dies.

**18** Complete the sentences with the correct names.

**Miller The Predator Lex**

**a)** ... shoots at the Aliens' eggs with a gun.

**b)** ... throws a bomb into the room with the Aliens' eggs.

**c)** ... is the only person from the team who lives.

**19** What do you think?

**a)** What will Lex do now?

**b)** What is going to happen on the Predator ship?

## NEW WORDS!

**What do these words mean?**

alien (n) ............................

bomb (n) ............................

chain (n) ............................

flare (n) ............................

helicopter (n) ............................

helmet (n) ............................

hunt (v) ............................ / hunter (n) ............................

ice (n) ............................

machine (n) ............................

predator (n) ............................

pyramid (n) ............................

rope (n) ............................

satellite (n) ............................

shoot (v) ............................

sled (n) ............................

space (n) ............................

spear (n) ............................

tail (n) ............................

tunnel (n) ............................

weapon (n) ............................